STRANGE STAINS AND MYSTERIOUS SMELLS

STRANGE
STAINS
AND
MYSTERIOUS
SMELLS

TERRY JONES & BRIAN FROUD

QUENTIN COTTINGTON'S JOURNAL OF FAERY RESEARCH

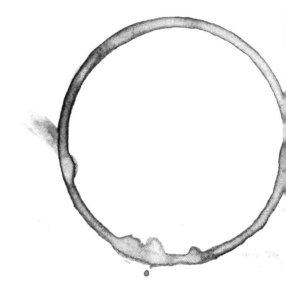

SIMON & SCHUSTER EDITIONS
Rockefeller Center
1230 Avenue of the Americas
New York, New York 10020

Design and Art Direction by Fiona Andreanelli and David Costa at *Wherefore* ART?

SIMON & SCHUSTER EDITIONS and colophons are trademarks of Simon & Schuster Inc.

1 3 5 7 9 10 8 6 4 2

Library of Congress Cataloging-in-Publication Data

Jones, Terry, 1942–
    Strange stains and mysterious smells : based on Quentin
Cottington's Journal of Faery Research / by Terry Jones & Brian
Froud.
        p.   cm.
    1. Faeries--Humor.   I. Froud, Brian.   II. Title.
PN6231.F283J66   1996
398'.0207--dc20
                                                                            96-8891
                                                                               CIP

ISBN 0-684-83206-2

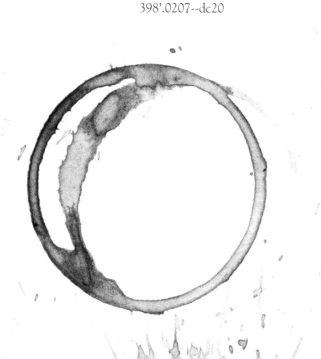

PREFACE

IN THE WAKE OF THE EXTRAORDINARY AND NOW FAMOUS *LADY COTTINGTON'S PRESSED FAERY BOOK*, COMES THE SENSATIONAL DISCOVERY OF HER HITHERTO UNKNOWN TWIN BROTHER QUENTIN'S OWN JOURNAL. TERRY JONES AND BRIAN FROUD, DURING ONE OF THEIR FREQUENT PERIODS OF UNEMPLOYMENT, HAD TAKEN UP FORMATION FLOWER-ARRANGING, AND WHILST CUTTING PEONIES IN THE GARDENS OF THE INSTITUTE FOR THE CRIMINALLY INSANE, THEY CHANCED UPON A LARGE TIN BOX BURIED IN THE GARDEN. ITS CONTENTS PROVED QUITE REMARKABLE.

At first sight all it contained were a few pieces of rusting, scientific equipment whose purpose was unknown. However, in the bottom of the box was a mildewed book, which turned out, on inspection, to be nothing less than a journal of scientific experiments, kept by Quentin Cottington, during his stay in the above mentioned Institute*. Not only did the book record every experiment carried out by Quentin, it also included detailed instructions concerning the use and maintenance of the equipment.

It appears that while his twin sister, Angelica Cottington, was obsessed by faeries, Quentin was obsessed by the seamy world of stains and blotches, smears and maculations, specks, smirches, marks, blemishes, spatters, daubs and blots of all kinds. He was equally curious about smells. He became convinced that both stains and smells possess a life of their own; that they are living entities capable of thought and reproduction. He therefore begged and cajoled his hosts at the Institute for the Criminally Insane to provide him with the means of constructing the equipment he needed to pursue his theory.

With the aid of a grant from the F.E.H.P.A.C.I. (Foundation For the Encouragement of Harmless Pursuits Amongst The Criminally Insane), Quentin Cottington constructed his "Psychic Image Nebulising Generator" and his "Primary Odour Nasalising Gasificator". He then devoted thirty years of painstaking scientific research to revealing the true nature of stains and smells.

Why he never communicated his results to the world is still a mystery. Perhaps, having seen the ridicule and scorn showered upon his sister, upon publication of her first 'faery photograph', he chose not to risk exposing himself to similar contempt. Perhaps he felt the world was not yet ready

---

* The Institute For the Criminally Insane is a fine example of privatised health care - catering not only to the Criminally Insane but also to those seeking a stress-free holiday in quiet yet amusing and constantly surprising surroundings. Why not book your holiday today? One of our "Away-From-It-All" weekends can cost as little as $120 per person or a Deluxe Euro-Executive Weekend For Two enticingly priced at $550 including use of the secure wing.

for such startling revelations. Perhaps he himself found it difficult to accept the startling results of his experiments. But whatever the reason, Quentin Cottington remained silent about his remarkable discoveries and shortly before his death, buried all his equipment and his journal in the garden of the Institute for The Criminally Insane, where they remained, until Terry Jones and Brian Froud chanced upon them.

Inspired by Quentin Cottington's scientific approach, Jones and Froud were able to restore the Cottington equipment to full running order. They then set about repeating the experiments as recorded in Quentin's journal. The results were staggering.

With the aid of the "Psychic Image Nebulising Generator" they were able to reveal for the first time in history, the true nature of the spots and stains that surround us in daily life. Similarly the "Primary Odour Nasalising Gasificator" analysed the "etheric protoplasmic nature" of smells. By using these two pieces of apparatus Jones and Froud found they could reveal the corporeal existence - normally invisible to the human eye - of stains and smells. Unfortunately these images proved too insubstantial to be recorded photographically. Brian Froud therefore set about the immense task of painting each one of them as they were discovered. In the meantime, Terry Jones interviewed these strange and hitherto totally unknown creatures. The result is this astonishing book.

Here is a full and unexpurgated guide to The Unnatural History of Mess-Makers and Pong-Perpetrators, in which we are able to see for the first time, the fascinating creatures that create and that <u>are</u> *Strange Stains and Mysterious Smells*.

Quentin Cottington
A Brief Memoir

IT WILL COME as a complete surprise to any reader of *Lady Cottington's Pressed Faery Book* that Lady Cottington should have possessed a twin brother. Nothing in her diaries nor anything she said, ever gave the least hint that such a sibling existed. The reason for this silence will probably never be known. Was Angelica Cottington ignorant of his existence or did she simply choose to ignore it?

It is certainly possible that a wet-nurse, who was employed by the family for a short time after the birth, could have spirited the infant away in an attempt to blackmail the family. Neither parent would have noticed such a loss, since the pressing engagements of a full social diary and the formidable pressures of being seen in the right restaurants often meant that it was impossible to keep a full tally of all one's children. Indeed, given the atmosphere of ignorance and taboo in which affairs such as birth and death were conducted at that time, it is even probable that the then Lady Cottington was unaware that she had given birth to twins. There is, however, no record of any blackmail attempt.

The possibility that Angelica suppressed the knowledge of her twin brother's existence begs the question: why? What was so dreadful about this sibling? What triggered her displeasure?

A doctor writes: "sibling enmity often starts in the womb. Especially when the embryos are of different sexes. Failure of the male embryo to allow the female to leave the womb first or make sure she is sitting comfortably during the nine months of gestation can damage any chance of a relationship through the remainder of their lives. Similarly refusal of the female embryo to join in a game of football before birth can traumatize the male and mark him for life." But all this is speculation - some might say worthless speculation at that. In any case the doctor who wrote it was not a real doctor and has since been imprisoned for impersonating a police officer.

The real question is what was this twin brother like? What sort of a man was he? Did he use safety matches or those ones with red tips? Why did he remain concealed and unacknowledged for so long? What was his phone number?

Now at last a chance discovery has placed in our hands a document that sheds light on at least twelve of these questions. It is nothing less than a complete autobiography of Quentin Cottington. Unfortunately it is written in an indecipherable hand (possibly Venusian) and a complete transcription is impossible. Before his death in a chopping accident, however, I was privileged to hear a reading of the complete text by the the author's closest friend: a well-respected family butcher by the name of Hans the Venusian. What follows is a memoir compiled from the notes I took over many happy days sitting on Hans' chopping block listening to him read.

QUENTIN COTTINGTON
ANOTHER BRIEF MEMOIR

QUENTIN COTTINGTON was obsessed with hygiene. Even at an early age he washed his hands and even washed behind his ears, every time anyone said the word: "bilious", which, as he suffered from an incommoding gastric ailment, was rather often.

As an adult he would take a bath at the drop of a hat. Every time a glove was dropped he would take a shower. If a pair of gloves, a hat and some of Wordsworth's pottery* were dropped in rapid succession he would immerse himself in scalding hot water and refuse to come out until someone said the word "frugal".

It is said that he washed his hands over two thousand times a day - possibly as a result of his unshakeable conviction that water was inherently dirty. This meant that after every ablution he had to wash the water off and then wash that off and so on and so on.

Concerning the accident of his birth and his estrangement from the Cottington family, Quentin always remained resolutely silent. If questioned on the subject he would mutter "Angelica stank" and refuse to speak another word until someone said the word "lamppost". He was obsessed with the repetition of certain words and the possible effect the pattern of such repetition might have on interstellar communication.

At the age of sixteen, he began to suffer from a little-known disease which is somewhat akin to rising damp in buildings. His property value declined and, in the course of his search for a cure, he consulted several award-winnng architects. Eventually he was declared not only rot-free but had a complete guaranteed damp-course installed and a family of hairdressers living in his waistband.

On leaving school, he went round the corner and bought an ice-cream before going on to Oxford, where he studied Science under the world-renowned Prof. Herman Hesse. It was here, under Prof. Hesse, that he first discovered the world of stains and smells that was to preoccupy him for the rest of his short life.

The underside of Prof. Hesse was, indeed, already world-renowned as a breeding-site of outstanding richness and bio-diversity. The World Wild Life Institute proclaimed his bottom a PSSI (Place of Special Scientific Interest) and his groin was declared a World Wildlife Nature Reserve in 1909. But it was Prof. Hesse's trousers that particularly fascinated the young Quentin Cottington. Here he found stains of a richness and a variety that he had never come across before. He became obsessed by their origins, causes and nature.

---

* It is a little known fact that Willliam Wordsworth, besides being a major English poet, also crafted some of the most sought-after dishwasher-proof dinner-ware in Nineteenth Century literary circles.

For him a stain was not simply a random mark on the surface of the material world. "Stains," he wrote in one of the few personal communications he made that was not in Venusian, "are living things. They have a life, a character and a destiny. Every stain has a story to tell. And it will be my life's work to tell that story."

Quentin Cottington devoted the rest of his life to opening up the world of stains. In 1910 he extended his investigations to include smells, odours, redolences, emanations, exhalations, whiffs, fumes, pungencies, fetors, stenches, reeks, mephitises, miasmata and stinks.

His family were convinced he was mad. Indeed he was locked away in the Institute for the Criminally Insane after recklessly trying to examine a stain on the then Princess Royal's 'Jockey' briefs. He eventually died of food-poisoning shortly after a visit by his sister in 1939.

The World had written off his life as a waste of time. That is until the discovery of his apparatus and journals. Terry Jones and Brian Froud take up the story.

THE DISCOVERY OF
QUENTIN COTTINGTON'S JOURNAL
BY TERRY JONES & BRIAN FROUD

HELLO, I'M TERRY JONES. And I'm Brian Froud. You can tell which of us is writing at any particular moment by the simple, but we hope effective device, that when I'm writing (*this is Terry Jones*) I will use the word "heelpost". Whereas when I'm writing (*this is Brian Froud*) I will always put inverted commas around any word beginning with 'x'. I hope this is clear enough (*NB: no use of the word "heelpost" in this sentence! Get it?*) And I hope you will be able to guess who is writing this bit (*unfortunately there was no word beginning with 'x' in that particular sentence, but if there had have been, it would have been in inverted commas - so you ought to know who is writing this!*)

Brian and I were rummaging around the door of the shed, in the gardens of the Institute for the Criminally Insane, when we came across a small cavity by the heelpost… (*all right I know I said I wouldn't use the word 'heelpost' when I was writing so you could distinguish my sentences from Brian's, but in this particular case there is simply no other word for 'the post of a door or gate which carries the hinges' - and in any case I started the sentence off with the words 'Brian and I' so it would be quite obvious to anyone but a total imbecile who it was who was writing this particular sentence. In any case does it 'x-actly' matter who is writing at any particular time, Terry? No, Brian, I don't suppose it does, and, since you mention it, it's not 'exactly' good spelling having to writing 'exactly' as 'x-actly' just so that… Look, Terry, why don't we start again, without having to distinguish between who is writing what at any given time? Good idea, Brian*).

THE DISCOVERY
OF QUENTIN COTTINGTON'S JOURNAL
BY TERRY JONES AND BRIAN FROUD
{written jointly by two writers and without
attempting to distinguish the one from the other.}

IT WAS A BRIGHT spring morning. We (that is the two joint-authors) were digging around the garden shed of the Institute for the Criminally Insane, when we discovered by the *heelpost [NB the inclusion of this word does not imply a sentence written only by Brian Froud]* an object at a depth of about six feet. "It is an object at depth of about six feet," said Brian Froud. *[Author's Note: I (that is Terry Jones) don't think we need that last sentence. Personally I think it holds up the interesting narrative and is merely repeating what had already been stated in the previous sentence. As far as I can see Brian merely wants it included so that he gets all the credit for making the Discovery. Another Author's Note: This is a total misrepresentation of the facts. Editor's Note: Will the Authors please stop bickering and get on with the interseting narrative? Otherwise there will be no royalty statement until the end of next year.]*

THE DISCOVERY
OF QUENTIN COTTINGTON'S JOURNAL
BY TERRY JONES & BRIAN FROUD
{As told to their Editor}

WE WERE BOTH DIGGING in the garden of the Institute for the Criminally Insane, when *simultaneously* our spades struck on something hard. "Perhaps this is the Discovery of a Lifetime!" we both exclaimed *simultaneously*. Within a few minutes we had uncovered a rusting tin box that had probably, at one time, contained biscuits or cream crackers. Froud was of the opinion that it may have once contained a Huntley and Palmer Variety Assortment, but Jones inclined to the theory that it was more likely to have been a Peak Frean Tea-Time Creams tin; although after some debate they both agreed that it could also possibly have been a Jacobs Assorted Crackers tin from around 1932. It was certainly similar in shape to the McVitie Morning Coffee Assortment although the metal itself was more like that used by the Royale Biscuit Company at the turn of the…

{*Can we please get on with the interesting narrative - Ed.*}

In a trice we had opened the tin and discovered that it contained two strange pieces of apparatus of no known use and a book. "Perhaps the book will tell us what the apparatus of no known use is for!" we both exclaimed *simultaneously*. In a trice we had opened the book and both *simultaneously* recognized the hand of Quentin Cottington. On the very first page was a detailed description of the scientific equipment and an equally detailed description of the manner of its construction. Using this as a guide, we both reconstructed and renovated the apparatus. We were then able to follow the detailed instructions on how to wear it and on its use.

The first piece of apparatus, APPARATUS A, as we called it, proved to be the "PSYCHIC IMAGE NEBULISING GENERATOR". Froud wore this over his eyes and nose while Jones put the apparatus known as APPARATUS B, over his mouth and nose. This was the "PRIMARY ODOUR NASALISING GASIFICATOR".

Our first experiments, however, proved a disappointment, and it was only when we started to peruse the journal itself that we learned the correct adjustments and precise alignment necessary for their functioning.

In his *Journal of Experiments* Quentin Cottington describes how his first investigation was directed towards a a small stain on the front of his shirt. Since Froud had plenty of similar stains as the result of a curry he had eaten the previous evening, we decided to follow suit. Froud donned the "PSYCHIC IMAGE NEBULISING GENERATOR" and Jones wore the "PRIMARY ODOUR NASALISING GASIFICATOR". Painstakingly we followed step-by-step the experiment as described on page five of the Journal.

The stain was isolated in a brightish patch of sunlight and activated by application of the *Macule-Energizing Vector* (usually a lump of mild cheese such as Caerphilly or Double Gloucester placed within the radius of odour). The *etheric antenna* was given its final tuning and the *protoplasmic locating resonator* was brought into play. Froud adjusted the *nebulising generator focussing mechanism* while Jones applied the *nasalising gasificator induction canopy* directly to the spot. We waited with bated breath. This was the test. Would Quentin Cottington prove to have been the pioneer who first put the Human World in touch with the hidden spirits of the World of Olefaction and Maculation? or would his thirty years of painstaking scientific research proved to have been but the delusions of a Criminally Insane mind?

We stood there for several hours, waiting with the patience that only those who have known the thrill of pure scientific investigation can understand. Nothing happened.

The sun was getting low on the horizon and we were both thinking it would be best to leave the scientific experiment for today and try again tomorrow, when we both *simultaneously* noticed a small brass node on the side of each piece of equipment. I looked at Froud and I looked at

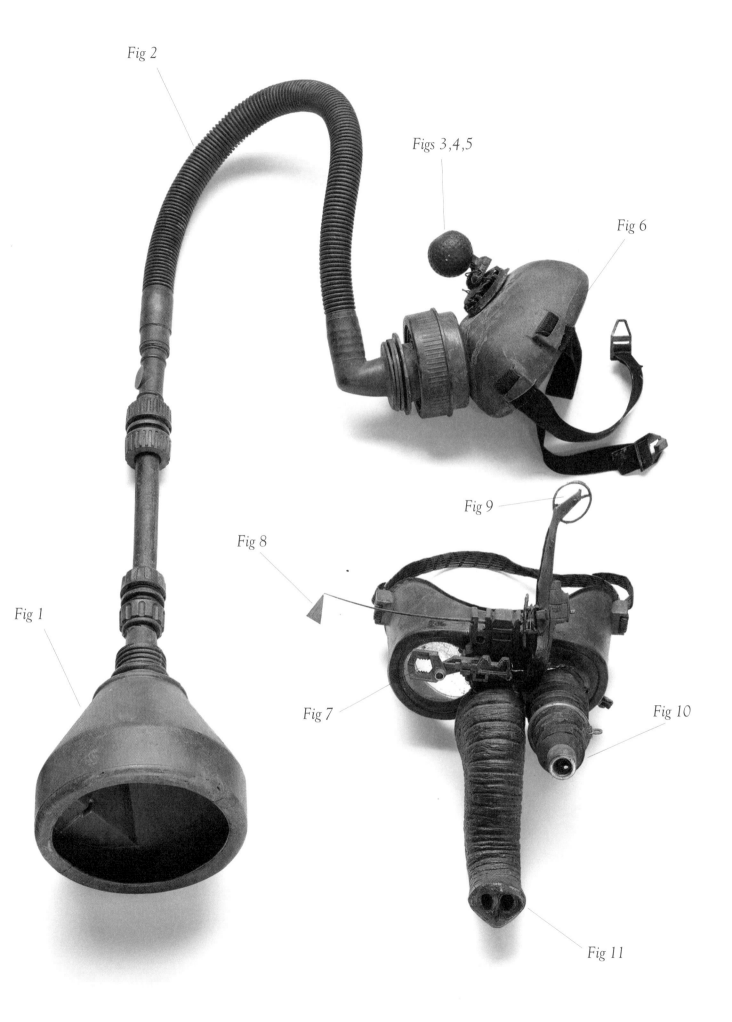

Fig 2

Figs 3,4,5

Fig 6

Fig 9

Fig 8

Fig 1

Fig 7

Fig 10

Fig 11

Jones. We both *simultaneously* realised that these experiments were going to be trickier than we had at first thought. Every detail had to be just right. We had forgotten to switch the machines on.

The moment we flicked the two switches to the "on" positions, we stared with incredulity at what we saw: nothing. Even switching the damn things on didn't do any good! Clearly the man was mad. We had just resolved not to waste any more time on pursuing the fantasies of a deranged mind... when one of us sneezed. In a second there in front of us, where the stain had been on Froud's shirt, was a small purple creature with delicate ears and four toes.

In retrospect it is clear that Quentin had deliberately under-powered both the Generator and the Gasificator. His Journal constantly mentions "the secret force" and the "certain something" which were the "key" to operating his machines. The concentrated energy released by the act of sneezing had pushed the energizing power pack beyond the critical mass. Quentin Cottington's last secret was revealed - his "secret power" was nothing less than the simple Sneeze.

For a moment neither of us could speak. Then, before we could even reach for a handkerchief, the stain or creature spoke.

"I'm sorry," it said. "I shouldn't be here."

Now this was something neither of us had bargained for. The optical manifestation of the stain was in itself a staggering achievement, but here we were faced with the prospect of making aural contact as well.

"What do you mean - you 'shouldn't be here'?" asked Jones.

"You don't know what it's like," replied the creature, "having to sit all hours of the day exposed to the prying eyes of all and sundry. It's a terrible life on a shirt front. Not like some - who get it nice and warm, hidden away for weeks in someone's underpants - oh no! I'm paraded round on the front of shirts for all to see and snigger at. I hate my life.'

We looked at each other. We had made history. From now on, we would be able not only to record the visual evidence of the life of stains but also investigate their life stories as well. For the next year, we devoted ourselves to completing the work which Quentin Cottington began. We located and interviewed over seven hundred and eighty stains and odours. The results of as many of these strange encounters as are fit to print are contained in this book.

We hope you will share with us the thrill and fascination of discovering the world of Strange Stains and Mysterious Smells.

TERRY JONES & BRIAN FROUD
LONDON & CHAGFORD,
JANUARY 1996

EXTRACTS FROM
QUENTIN COTTINGTON'S JOURNAL

1 THE THEORETICAL STRUCTURES OF STAINS.

[NB some of the marks on this page are believed to be part of Quentin Cottington's lunch and are not directly related to the scientific study itself.]

2 OPTICAL AUGMENTATION AND PRESSURE OF PARTLY-REMOVED STAINS.

Once he realised that stains were living creatures, Quentin Cottington devoted much care and research into the protection of the species. The depredations of dry-cleaners and laundries were, as he saw it, a constant threat to this sometimes embattled genius and he exerted much effort in his attempt to preserve and save as many of them as possible.

3 PRIMARY ODOUR NASALISING GASIFICATOR (PROTOTYPE)

Though this device lacks many of the refinements such as the *Pan-Mephitic Analysing Decoder* or the *Olfaction Dialysis Chamber* it can be clearly recognised, nevertheless, as a true Gasificator, embodying, as it does, the basic system which Quentin Cottington used to detect and metamorphose smells. Note the rudimentary corporealization of the Mid-Whiff [Fig.1]. The Gasificator Prototype has succeeded in manifesting a crude approximation of the creature - but appears to have lacked the power and focussing refinement to create more than an elaborate blob on the paper. Many more trials and experiments lay ahead of Quentin Cottington before his dream was to be fulfilled.

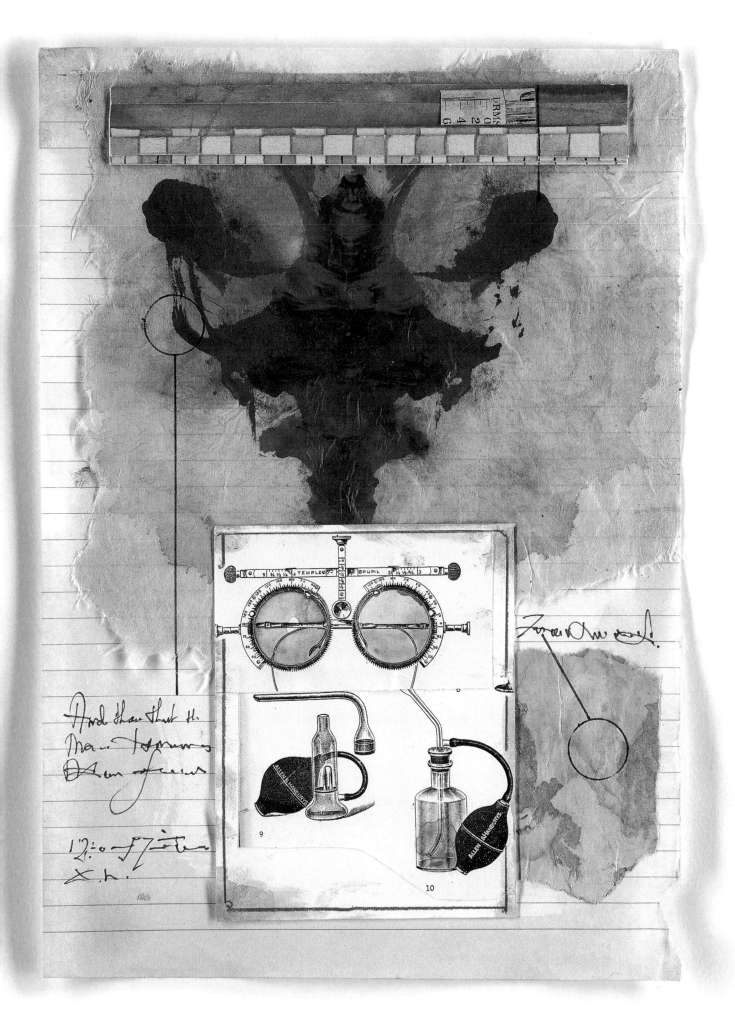

Pl.i

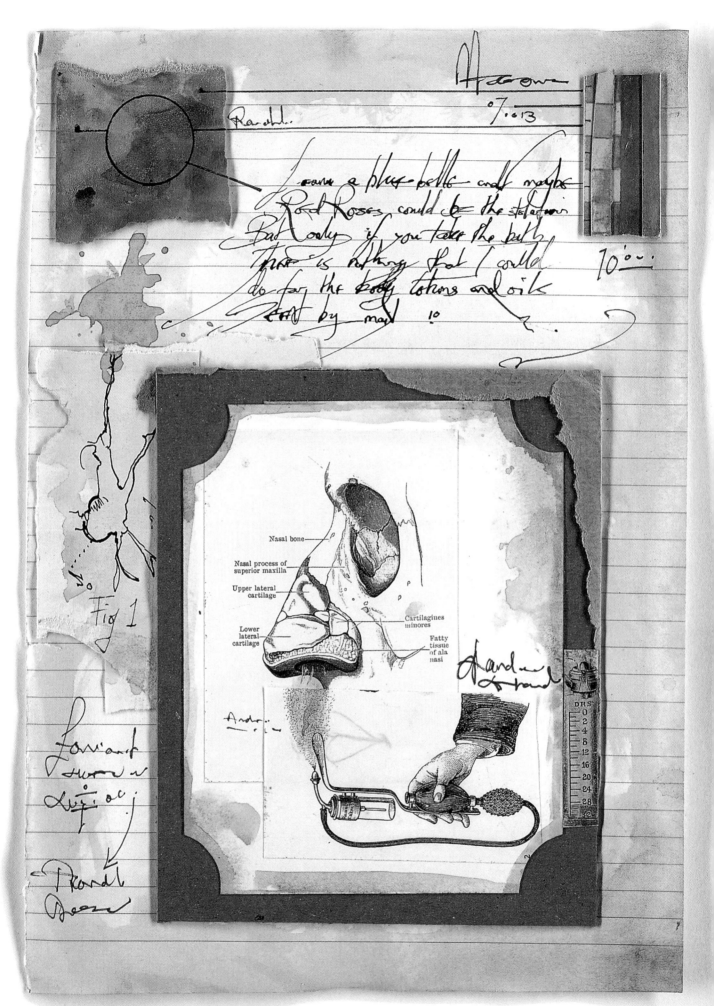

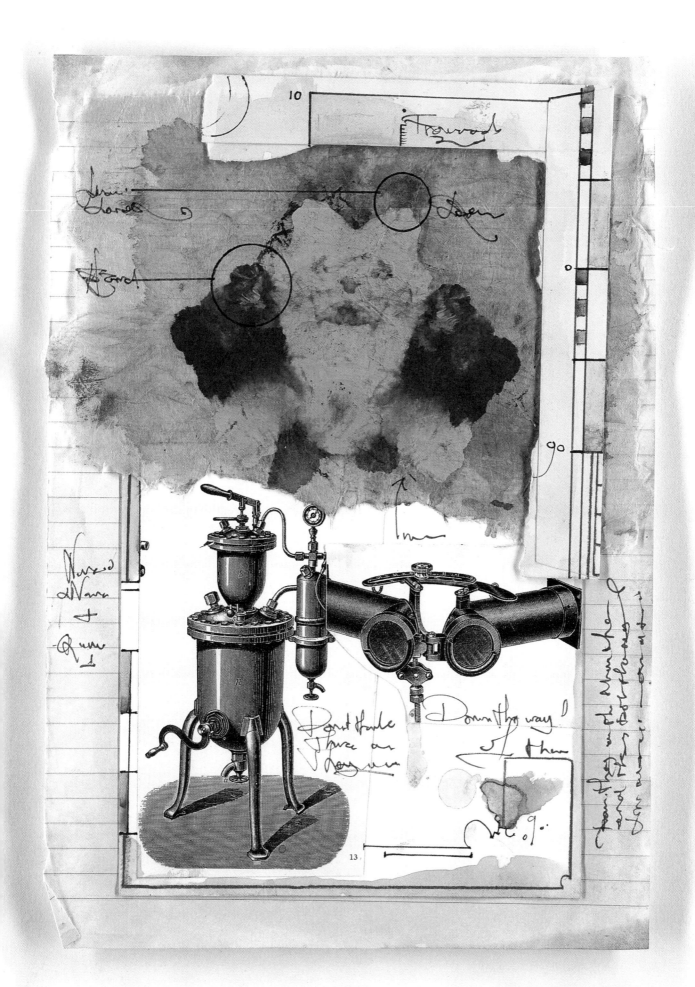

BULE KETTY

This was our first successful corporealization. The **Bule Ketty,** as the creature claimed to be called, inhabits the front of shirts. Usually it is a complete mystery how it got there, and the **Bule Ketty** itself can provide little information on its manner of arrival. The presence of wings, however, suggests some form of flight.

The **Bule Ketty** is not happy with its lot. It finds the life of constant exposure on the shirt-front onerous and it envies the sort of stains who live in hidden recesses such as armpits and on underclothes. When we asked why it didn't choose some other habitat, the **Bule Ketty** merely sulked and said "as it didn't know how it got there in the first place, it didn't know how to get off from there," and it accused us of being "prying ignoramuses who didn't know the first thing about the life of stains".

Despite its prominent position, the **Bule Ketty** can be surprisingly long-lived and can be spotted on almost any male human — even prominent politicians are not immune from her visits — especially after state banquets and heavy luncheons with the Press.

Pl.iv Bule KETTY

WHOOPER THE SCOT

This northern stain inhabits the fringes of kirtles and the undersides
of skilly-pans. Porridge when half-cooked and flicked with a wooden
spoon across the kitchen gives a fair approximation of **Whooper The Scot**,
but, of course, it is not be the real thing. **Whooper** hails from the
rain-swept moors of Glencoe, across the heath-covered fells and lowlands
he wanders, choosing here a lowly cot and there a grand mansion to play
his jokes and bring his pipes and reels. For this is no dour **Scot**.
Whooper is a Dancing Stain, a fun-loving, rib-poking joker of a Stain.
He loves nothing more than to leave a slippery trail and then watch the
folk slide and whoop as they execute the intricate dances that he has
assigned them.

    Whooper tells of mist-filled twilights, sitting round the fireside
of Robbie Burns, helping the great poet shell peas.

    "Robbie was crazy about peas," recalls **Whooper the Scot**. "He just
loved the feel of the pod and then clicking it open and finding all the
little round green buds inside and scooping them out with his thumb. He
never ate them – he was too much of a gentleman for that, but he loved
to shell them."

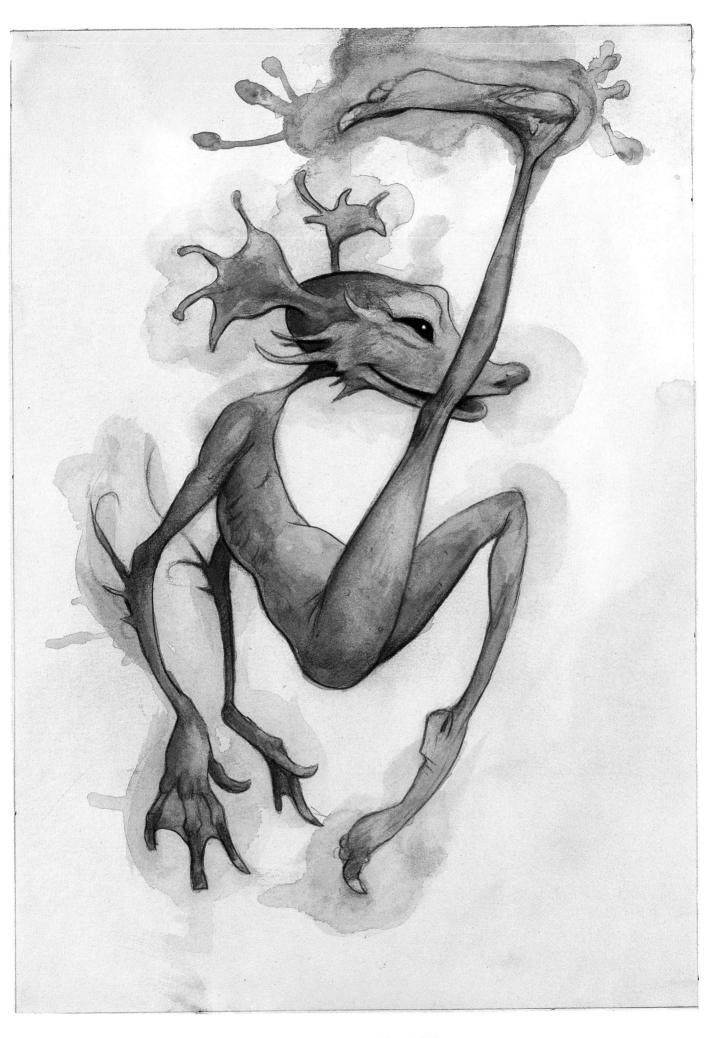

Pl.v Whooper The SCOT

MAI TEE PONG GENUS: JOCIS TERRIBILIS

Perhaps one of the least pleasant odours we had to encounter. **Mai** normally inhabits the interior of cylindrical cans on which are inscribed the misleading words: "Floral Air Freshener". Anyone foolish enough to press the button marked 'press' releases **Mai** into the atmosphere, thereby not only depleting the increasingly scarce ozone layer above our planet, but also filling the room with an indescribable noxious stench which bears about as much similarity to "Floral Air" as Newt Gingrich does to George Washington. As for the "Freshener" bit - this is merely the product of a deranged mind and not to be taken seriously.

Mai is capable of making even the most delicate of fastidious diners prefer to eat ~~their own vomit~~ **someone else's phlegm** rather than stay in the same room. And yet, curiously, the cans in which she hides are sold openly over the counter, and good money continually changes hands for the privilege of dispersing this dreadful malodour into the atmosphere. We became convinced that **Mai** must exert some subliminal influence over potential customers that forces them to buy the cans despite the dread contents. We were of the opinion that she sings a siren song at a pitch inaudible to the human ear, but which nonetheless affects the *Central Cranial Emptional Nerve* (that part of the human brain that controls the urge to buy things). We were, however, unable to test our theory or question her about it owing to the fact that we were overcome with the fumes and were forced to discontinue the experiment.

Pl.vi Mai Tee PONG (GENUS: JOCIS TERRIBILIS)

MATRICULUS MYGHELANGELICUS

When we first corporealized this stain, it refused to speak. It simply grinned and started waving its arms around. After a while we realised what it was doing. It was painting. It is, indeed, one of the most creative and artistically prolific stains in existence. It is easily recognized in the field, by the fact that at first sight one is inclined to believe it is not a stain but a deliberate work of art. For example on a plain T-Shirt it will at first appear as a design – perhaps featuring Hillary Clinton or part of Arnold Schwarzenegger. On closer inspection, however, it turns out to be a rather nasty patch of something that had once been in someone's stomach.

When we finally managed to draw its life story out of the **Matriculus Myghelangelicus**, it told us a tale of Papal Courts and Venetian Palazzos, of sunny days lounging on Tuscan floors, of long hard winters spent decorating village walls in Lombardy. "Ah, we lived well in those days," he told us. "Princes gave me their leave to brighten the town of Umbria and the gardeners of Fiesole welcomed me into their bowers to brighten the skirts of maids of honour. But then came the evil hour, when the Tyrant of Pisa had me banished from my native land. I was forbidden to be seen with lord or peasant, and I had to flee to these bitter and freezing northern lands, where scarce a single soul really appreciates my work."

He then began to weep copious tears, and we were forced to turn off our machine and move onto the next.

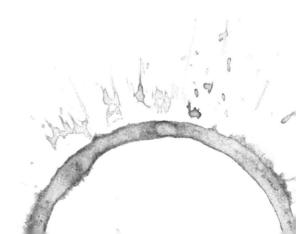

Pl.vii Matriculus MYGHELANGELIOUS

MEGGO (Genus: Jocunda Innoxia Temporabilis)

This was one of those stains that, when you see it, causes you to say to yourself: **"Oh well, that's not too bad."** It's the kind of stain you might acquire from eating sushi - really nothing to worry about, unless you've over-done the soy sauce. In short it's the sort of stain you just don't mind having.

It was little surprise that when we turned the "Image Nebulising Generator" onto this subject, it should turn out to be such a carefree little thing as **Meggo** (of the genus: *Jocunda innoxia temporabilis*). Here is a transcript of the interview that followed.

T.J.: May I ask you a few questions?

MEGGO: Whoops! Nearly slid off the bath!

(We were interviewing in a bathroom)

T.J.: What is your favourite pastime?

MEGGO: You're a cutie!

T.J.: Can you tell us something about your life?

MEGGO: Nothing to tell. Nothing to hide. What you see is what you get! Whoops! That was the longest slide yet - wasn't it? I'm so happy to meet you, handsome!

T.J.: Look I don't think you ought to climb onto my sleeve...

MEGGO: What's wrong? Don't you like me? Is there something wrong with me? Do you think I'm ugly?

T.J.: No, no! You're fine.

MEGGO: You're a cutie.

T.J.: Ah well, now you're on my sleeve I suppose you might as well stay there.

MEGGO: Oh! I do hope we're going to get along. I really love being on you're sleeve.

T.J.: Yeah. Fine. Look, Brian, we might as well get onto the next stain.

B.F.: Don't you want to...you know...clean that sleeve off?

MEGGO: Oh! You wouldn't be so cruel!

T.J.: It'll be alright. It's not too bad.

MEGGO: You're a cutie.

Pl.viii Meggo (GENUS: JOCUNDA INNOXIA TEMPORABILIS)

THE EPIZOOTIC ZYMOT

One of the most rabid and unhelpful stains with which we came into contact during our researches. It is one of the few stains that is capable of fighting back against Laundries and Dry Cleaners. It has been known to spread marmalade on the soles of its tormentors' shoes and even - on occasion - to have reported innocent laundromat owners to the police for employing under-aged handkerchiefs. **The Epizootic Zymot** is characterized by its ability to replicate itself when attacked. It is one of those mysterious stains that as soon as you try to clean it off one bit of the table-cloth it immediately appears on another. The more you try and remove it the more places it reappears.

Best to leave this one alone.

...plete surprise to any reader of Lady Cottington's Pressed Faery Book that Lady Cottington should have possessed a twin brother. Nothing in her diaries nor anything she said, ever gave the least hint that such a sibling existed. The reason for this silence will probably never be known. Was Angelica Cottington ignorant

...pry c... ...ignore it!

It is certainly possib... that a wet-nurse who, w... employed by the family for... short time after the birth... could have spirited the infant... away in an attempt to black... mail the family. Neither par... ent would have noticed such... loss, since the pressing engag... ments of a full social diary a...

Pl.ix The Epizootic ZYMOT

THE NOXIMORON

This is one of those smells that suddenly and boldly manifests itself whenever two or more humans are driving in a car. Everyone looks at everyone else, secretly, trying to decide who is responsible. Usually it is conveniently blamed on the dog, who has been sleeping soundly throughout the journey. It is a very stubborn smell and refuses to budge even when all the car windows are opened. The truth, as we discovered after several hours of interviewing, is that the Noximoron enjoys cars and has merely come along for the ride. It is usually on its way to a more prestigious occasion, such as a Royal Investiture or the Moderator of the General Assembly of the Church of Scotland's dinner table.

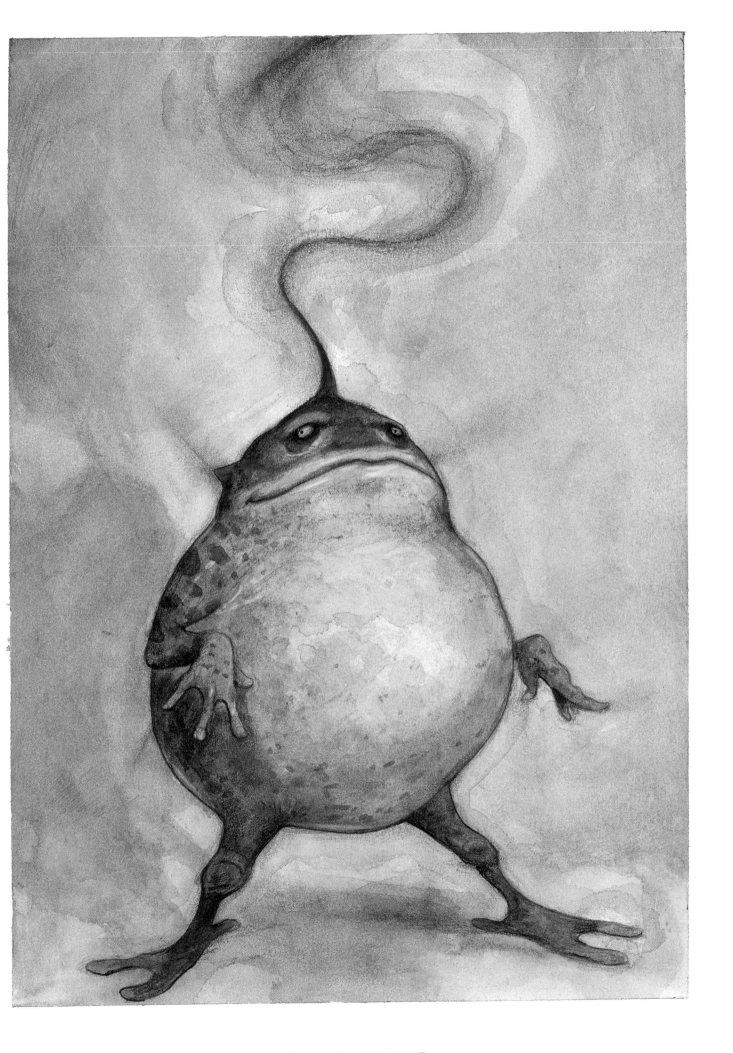

Pl.x The NOXIMORON

MELDRIPPER PESTILENSIS

Once we had approached the **Meldripper** for an interview we found it was very difficult to stop him talking. He is one of those stains that happens totally without apparent cause, when you are laughing. Something really tickles your ribs, you laugh, uncontrollably perhaps, for say thirty seconds, and then as you regain your composure, you find there is a long streak of something slimey down your front and over the desk.

We asked the **Meldripper** how he got where he does without being seen, but his reply consumed three or four notebooks of transcript and seemed to be comprised of an endless story about a man taking a dog that had a lot of hair on it for a walk on a winter's night. He then told us several one-liners which are unrepeatable and blew his nose all over our fronts.

We decided to terminate the experiment in the interests of

hygiene.

Pl.xi   Meldripper PESTILENSIS

VLAD THE INHALER

An unlikely name for an unlikely smell. Descended from an ancient family
of hosiery from central Europe, **Vlad** migrated west and east, north and
south and is now found everywhere. He likes nothing better than to
settle down in the toe and heel of an old pair of socks. Totally
unperceived by the unsuspecting owner, he lurks in the socks and waits
for a choice moment to reveal himself, such as a visit to buy a new pair
of shoes, or, when about to leap into bed with the object of one's
desire, one kicks off one's shoes with gay abandon to be greeted by the
dreadful presence of **Vlad**.

"I cannot 'elp it," said **Vlad**. "It eez my destiny to be a
kill-joy, a marplot, a spoilsport, a wet blanket, a skeleton at ze
feast. My life! What a miserable existence! When I was no more
than a young whiff my mozzer, the Countess Von Schnozzle, held
great hopes for me – she dreamed of my becoming a big stink in ze
city or even a high pong at Court, but no! my damned fazzer, the
Count, he 'ated me. I do not know why he 'ated me, but he 'ated me
with a loathing that is unimaginable to anyone who has not been
loathed by their fazzer in that way. He wanted to ruin my life, so
he apprenticed me to a shoemaker and zat was zat. My mozzer, bless
her insoles, died of shame and grief. My damned fazzer took to the
bottle and died penniless. Ze family castle on ze Danube was put
up for auction to pay off his debts and I was forced to work for a
living. Eventually, when I became too old and feeble, I was zrown
into ze street without a ztitch of clozing nor a cruzt of bread.
Zus, wretch zat I am, I took to ze life I now lead – my zpeech
infezted with zeds ."

The miserable stench then heaved himself out of my sock and
shambled off down the road to find another quiet drawer where he could
sleep undisturbed for a few months more.

Pl.xii Vlad The INHALER

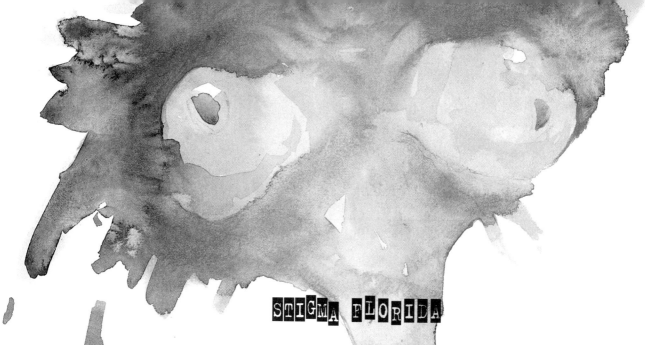

STIGMA FLORIDA

One of the old Celtic stains. "When the Romans first came to Briton," the **Stigma Florida** told us, " my family already had connections with the druids on Anglesey. We celebrated the Midwinter Festival and cut the mistletoe from the oak and apple. But the Romans brought a new religion with them, and I found plenty of work to do in Monasteries up and down England. Sometimes I would do no more than embarrass novitiates and younger monks, when the Abbot came to inspect their bed linen. But on occasions, I would create a sensation by appearing on the altar cloth, or some similar location, and then you would hear cries of: "A miracle! A miracle! The face of Jesus! It must be his shroud!" and so on. I would amuse myself in this way, until the unfortunate Abbot would invite his Archbishop to come and attest to the miracle. Then I would simply dis-appear. It helped to pass the time, you understand."

Whereupon the **Stigma Florida** vanished before our eyes.

Pl.xiii <u>Stigma FLORIDA</u>

LUCY LILO

A queer stain sprite who specializes in that seeming contradiction in terms; "*the invisible stain*". She produces a wonderful, rich and imaginative range of stains that you know are there, but the more you look at them the less you can see them. For example: you will take a suit jacket out of the wardrobe, examine its lapels carefully for any tell-tale remains of last week's dinner party or what happened after you went to the pub, and will see nothing. Not a speck. "Thank god!" you breathe a sigh of relief. "Perhaps I didn't throw up in the taxi after all!" So you are just slipping the suit on, when a Loved One enters and says:

"Surely!". Now in itself, 'surely' is not an intimidating word, but it is usually the harbinger of worse to come. Your heart sinks. The Loved One continues:

"Surely! You're not going to wear *that!*".
In a flash you know you've been caught by **Lucy Lilo** yet again.

"Wear what?" You try to brazen it out.

"That terrible stain on the lapel!" You look down and sure enough there is now the faint outline of a stain clearly visible.

And it's no good saying: "Oh! It's not so bad. I don't think anyone will notice," because you know, that if you were to wear it, **Lucy Lilo** will make the stain get bigger and bigger throughout the evening, so that, by the time you had found yourself chatting up that stunning girl in the corner whose father was the ex-Liberal MP for somewhere in the Highlands, it would look as if you just been sick down your jacket.

So you take the suit off again and yet, as you put it back into the cupboard, you re-examine the lapel, and sure enough! the stain is now almost invisible again. **Lucy Lilo** knows her business and works it well.

Pl.xiv Lucy LILO

PESTIFERUS POLLUTANS INOCULABILUS

A close cousin of the Epizootic Zymot (for which: see above) the **Pestiferus Pollutans** generally inhabits the sewers of Paris, where it has had a long and romantic history. It worked as a government spy during the Napoleonic Wars and was twice decorated by Bonaparte for its services. On the long march back from Moscow, the **Pestiferus Pollutans** went ahead of the troops to greet them at every village through which they passed. It was even rumoured that the Empress Josephine herself was somehow infatuated with it and would walk around with the stain proudly borne on one of her petticoats, but this may have been merely part of the black propaganda campaign waged by the English.

The **Pestiferus Pollutans** stayed with Napoleon through all his later trials and tribulations. At Waterloo, it is said to have been seen behind many soldiers on both sides. It finally accompanied the ex-Emperor to his exile on the isle of Elba, where it busied itself in decorating the latrines and privies of high and low, before returning to Paris.

An 18th Century Social Historian writes: "It is quite untrue that we 18th Century Social Historians are not computer-literate and still use old-fashioned pens. This is typical of the sort of propaganda churned out by the Thatcherite-Reaganite press of the 1980's and 90's who wish to see History written-out of the school syllabus so that more time can be devoted to 'Hotel Management' and 'First Steps in Asset-Stripping' etc. Their reason, of course, is that a knowledge of History is a tool that can be used against unscrupulous politicians. Knowledge of the Past helps the public of Today to make its own decisions about who should govern it, and enables it to see through the sound-bites and pap churned out by the spin-doctors and political managers who manipulate the modern media. As for the **Pestiferus Pollutans** I've never heard of it."

Pl.xv   Pestiferus Pollutans INOCULABILUS

PECKORY CUD

Amazingly under-funded, the **Peckory Cud** devotes his life to research into the effect of nasal extrusions on the material world. His main specializations are children's sleeves and artificial heart valves just before they are inserted into the patient - although he admits he has so far had considerably more success with the one than the other. "For some reason" he told us, "children nowadays don't seem to be interested in letting their noses run free as they used to. I blame television. I also blame Scud Missiles, but then what do I know? The research funds for my sort of scientific work gave out three thousand years ago. I write to the Institute of Nasal Extrusional Research every other century asking for further funds to carry out essential research in the field, but the Institute always writes back saying it doesn't exist. I then write back demanding how it the Institute can reply to my first letter if, as it claims, it doesn't exist. Three years later I usually get a short card saying my second letter has been noted and the contents will be passed on to the Institute of Nasal Extrusional Research if and when it decides it exists again. It's a depressing business."

The **Peckory Cud** is currently seeking funding from the Private Sector. "The big Multi-Nationals could really benefit from my sort of research," he claims. "For example I am currently trying to develop a nasal drip that eats into man-made fibres and causes severe skin burns - I mean that's the sort of thing that could interest both the clothing industry and private medicine. I have also produced a Special Nasally Originated Tastie (also known as S.N.O.T.) that could be used as a subsitute filling in most industrially-produced pork pies and cornish pasties - particularly those served in pubs and in low-light conditions. Anyway - I mean what's so wrong about eating S.N.O.T.? I mean to say - I've had to live off it for the last two and half millennia and it hasn't done me any harm! I love it! Boogers taste great! That's my slogan. 'Eat More Boogers And Less Children'! That's another slogan. 'Squigglies Of The World Untie!' That's another - although I'm thinking of changing that one to 'Squigglies Of The World Unite!' only it doesn't make quite such good sense.

"It really pisses me off how squeamish people are about what comes out of their noses. I mean we all eat leucorrhea and phlegm don't we? So what's so terrible about SNOT? I eat all I can get! It's great rolled up into a ball, sun-dried and served in truffle oil. I'm opening a SNOT restaurant - *Magret of Snot, Snot and Cinnamon Balls, Deep Fried Snot and Mushy Peas, Snot-in-a-Basket, Smoked Snot and Dill Sauce, Snot, Bogey and Squiggley Casserole*...Yum! Yum!"

The **Peckory Cud** was still talking as we excused ourselved and headed for the nearest vomitorium.*

Pl.xvi Peckory CUD

FLETTERA FLORALILLIA

Another smell sprite. **Flettera Floralillia** is the creator of all under-arm odours. Her work is probably most familiar to small boys as they are shown how to hold a basketball for the first time by Mr Simpson the Sportsmaster or to little girls who clamber into their mother's wonderbra, while she is in the shower after four hours in the shopping mall.

What is, perhaps, less well-known is the fact that **Flettera Floralillia** is obsessed by sex. In fact all the scents and aromas that she creates under our arms are directly aimed at sexual stimulation. **Flettera** is convinced that the under-arm area is the most erogenous of all zones and that it is enhanced by smells. "The male under-arm," she told us, "is a symbol of virility and power. I cannot understand why so many human beings cover-up their arm-pits or walk around with them squashed-up under their shoulders. Why don't they show them off more? I like to walk around with my arms up high – so that my arm-pits are exposed to the gaze of every faery who passes by. The female arm-pit is a beautiful area – secret and yet bold – full of yearning and the promise of safe harbour."

It was only when Brian Froud showed **Flettera** *his* arm-pit that I saw the slightest hesitation in her manner. Her face clouded slightly and she said, rather hesitatingly: "Are you sure that <u>is</u> your arm-pit, Mr Froud?"

However she recovered herself enough to leave us with this Ode To An Arm-Pit which she had just composed.

ODE TO AN ARM-PIT

Hidden garden of delight
Hairy hollow hid from sight
In your tangles there are charms
Buried underneath our arms.
Open up and face the light
Be proud! be free! proclaim your right
To show yourself for what you are:
Our body cavities' true star!

Pl.xvii Flettera FLORALILLIA

MEDULLA RECONDITA

A secretive smell that shuns the limelight and lies hidden, for sometimes years, in the navel. She usually hides under a covering of fluff and only emerges when this is removed by a finger or a bent paper-clip. **Medulla Recondita** is a particular favourite of children and art students, but seems to get on with most people. She is, however, surprisingly selective in her choice of hosts.

"Politicians - I like them," the **Medulla** told us. "They have warm moist navels, with fine amounts of fluff to keep me cosy. With them my days are spent, secure and happy, lulled by the occasional droning of their debates in the House, cheered by their long lunches and over-indulgent suppers at smart restaurants. Oh it's a good life, when I'm with a politician. And when bedtime comes we're never alone. There's always some warm partner to snuggle up against - usually a researcher or a member of the House of Lords. Then there's the long drive home to their constituencies and the recriminations from their wives and husbands - then I hugely enjoy the cowering and excuses - but, being politicians, their powers of invention never fail to provoke admiration from such a simple soul as I.

"Philosophers and academics, on the other hand, I do not enjoy. They are forever picking at me. They have unsocial hours and are often alone in bed. Their lot is not a happy one, and I try to avoid them as much as possible. The same with Turkish Restaurant owners and the Royal Ballet Corps. No! Give me a good mediocre politician and I'll show you a haven for for navel pongs like me."

Pl.xviii Medulla RECONDITA

SMURGLE

One of the most elusive smells in existence. The **Smurgle** moves quickly and silently and can change its nature at will. It is ~~XXXXis~~ one of the great pranksters of the World of Olfaction. A favourite pastime is to hover around TV studios just before the News. As soon as the Newsreader is on air, it insinuates itself under his or her desk making just enough odour to put the Newsreader off their Autocue. As soon as the bulletin is over, just as the Newsreader is complaining to the Studio Management, **Smurgle** changes into a pleasant scent of roses.

   Smurgle is also often found hanging around Flower-Shows and other agricultural Contests. Here he often settles on a vase of flowers and will give winter-flowering jasmine a scent not dissimilar to that of a Cairo urinal. **Smurgle** is, however, one of the few inhabitants of the World of Olfaction who has a social conscience, and he gives away huge sums of money to any good cause that has the word "Otter" in the title.

Pl.xix   <u>Smurgle</u>

GEORGE HACKENBUSH THE FOURTH

We questioned this stain persistently for over an hour about its name, but it still stuck to its story that it was called **"George Hackenbush IV"**. When we pointed out that it was a most unlikely name for a creature of its genus it merely replied: **"Why a duck?"** We tried to find out a little more about its life and habits but it would only say: **"I could dance with you till the cows come home. On second thought I'd rather dance with the cows till you came home."** It would then be convulsed in what appeared to be a coughing spasm or some sort of epileptic fit. It would gasp for air and its eyes stuck out on stalks and tears came down its cheeks.

We persisted with our questions. Could it tell us something about its family and background? **"Let's go somewhere where we can be alone,"** it replied. **"Ah! there doesn't seem to be anyone on this couch!"** Again this was followed by yet another spasm or fit.

Eventually we pointed out that we would be forced to abandon our enquiries if it refused to cooperate. **"Believe me,"** replied the **George Hackenbush IV, "you have to get up early if you want to get out of bed!"** Again it screwed up its face and began choking and coughing. We were just about to turn our attention elsewhere, when it stopped us: **"Listen,"** it said **" I wouldn't join any club that would have me as a member!"**

A FILM BUFF WRITES: Why this particular stain should have developed a fixation about Groucho Marx is not clear, but such fixations are by no means unusual. There is a case recorded of a patch of oil that thought it was Humphrey Bogart for several years, until it ended in tragedy when it tried to take up smoking. In the United States there are reports of kitchen grease marks going in for Elvis look-alike contests and winning.

Pl.xx George HACKENBUSH THE FOURTH

RODDY THE BIKER
real name: LENTIGO BICEPHALUS

The peculiar habitat of this stain is exclusively
NatWest ATM machines.
It is impossible to imagine how it ever gets there, but it does.
Sometimes it renders the plexi-glass display indecipherable,
sometimes it simply makes the keys sticky.
However it manifests itself,
its sole object is to prevent customers from doing their business.

"The NatWest never did me any favours,"

claims **Roddy The Biker,**
whose real name is Lentigo Bicephalus,

"so why should I do them any?
They got a lot of money.
I don't even have any pockets.
That's how poor I am.
So stuff them."

When we quizzed **Roddy the Biker** as to why he didn't
attack Barclay's Service Tills or the Midland Bank in the
same way he looked rather blank.

"Stuff you,"
he said.

"You come here with your arty-farty questions.
Well I never asked for this interrogation. So stuff you..."**

**The Editor writes: This is hardly any improvement. Please try to interview decent middle class stain sprites.

Pl.xxi Roddy The BIKER

KERBY EMESIS

A pavement stain.

It usually appears overnight and stretches itself out on the sidewalk to enjoy the sun, and watching people edge round it. It is, perhaps, one of the most persecuted stains in the world. "In Roman times," the **Kirby Emesis** told us, "they used to try and keep us off the streets, and confine us to special designated areas, but we always managed to break out on occasion - especially after three-day banquets or during some of Cicero's longer orations. Throughout history there has been a tradition of persecuting us. Why don't they let us use the pavement like everyone else?"

Conditions in London, however, have improved greatly for the **Kirby Emesis** over the last fifteen years or so. The closing down of London's Public Toilets and the cut-backs in local authority spending has meant that the **Kirby Emesis** has been able to flourish, unmolested on the streets of Britain's capital in a way that would have been unthinkable in the past. Now as we pick our way through the homeless of Piccadilly and the urine-rills of Soho, the **Kirby Emesis** is there to welcome us at every turn.

"Yes! I owe a lot to Lady Thatcher," claims the Kirby Emesis. "But for her ladyship, me and my family would never have enjoyed the freedom and longevity that we now do. God bless you, **Maggie! Long let us remain on London's streets - a proud and fitting memorial to all you have achieved!**"

Pl.xxii Kerby EMESIS

THE GANDERENE GILLYMANDER

The Ganderene Gillymander is one of the most benign of smell sprites. She is devoted to making feet smell delightful at all times - even after long hours in a pair of Dr. Schone's Patent Sandals For The Deaf* doing step-aerobics. Unfortunately the **Gillymander's** concept of a pleasant smell is not ours. She swoons over a three month old kipper; she goes into ecstasies if a dog's bottom is placed under her nose; she even enjoys some modern designer perfumes.

Hence our feet smell as they do. But **Ganderene Gillymander** would be heart-broken to know that all her loving efforts are unappreciated. She imagines she is winning a special place in the hearts of Human Beings. She told us of her hopes that we would one day celebrate her as we do the Tooth Fairy or the Fairy Godmother, and she dreams of a having a special statue erected to her in Kensington Gardens. "I would like it to celebrate all the beautiful foot-smells that I have created for the benefit of Mankind. Perhaps it could be covered over in raw sewage so it reminds folk of what I have done for their pedal extremities."

We felt it would have been unkind to disabuse so well-meaning a sprite and we left her still admiring the scent and flavour of her own big toe.

Editor's Note: After the interview Froud needed mouth-to-mouth resuscitation and Jones spent several days in hospital suffering from what was diagnosed as a mustard gas attack.

---

*Dr. Schone's Patent Sandals For The Deaf. These are indeed an invaluable aid for the hard-of-hearing. The Patent Sandal is worn in place of a normal shoe. When the wearer is approaching some object or impediment in their path a warning bell rings loudly and a recorded message in the right-hand sole says: "Warning! You are approaching a hazard. Take avoiding action by veering to the right or left as the case may be". For some reason, however, this eminently sensible piece of footwear has never been popular with the people for whom it was designed.

Pl.xiii The Ganderene GILLYMANDER

LOOBRITUS MECKANIKUS

This is stain is of uniquely mysterious origin. It appears without warning underneath parked cars. The man at the garage will swear blue the sump isn't leaking and the gaskets are fine but next time you park the car – there, underneath it again is **Loobritus Meckanikus.**

And it's no good trying to force him out from under – he simply won't budge. He is one of the most determined and obstinate of stains. The best way of dealing with him is to play any Des O'Connor record loud enough to blast him out from under the parked vehicle. ~~alike~~ Alternatively if the car is parked in the drive of your house, you could stand within earshot and pretend to be telling a neighbour that you've got Paul Daniels coming round for dinner that evening.

The **Loobritus** is actually an extremely vain creature. He prides himself on his powers as a popular entertainer and can't stand competition. We asked him to perform one of his Elvis look-alike performances and this was the result.

Pl.xxiv Loobritus MECKANIKUS

HOLMANOID KRANKENAUSENER PIFFNITCH

One of the few stains with a degree in psychology, **Holmanoid Krankenhausener Piffnitch** at first refused to be interviewed, but eventually agreed after we promised to balance a Nepalese Tree-Frog on our heads during the entire interview and let him touch our ball-point pens. He then got so excited that we had to call in his social-worker and a police-trained psychotherapist from Newbury whom he'd got attatched to on a train.

During the interview, **Holmanoid** kept asking for any bits of tinned fruit we might have secreted about our persons, and whether we could introduce him to any influential penguins. We eventually had to abandon the interview when **Holmanoid** tried to show us where he kept his pencils. We said we weren't writing that kind of book and he became extremely abusive. Froud received several blows to the brain, which he fortunately didn't notice, and Jones came away with an extended epiglottis which **Holmanoid** somehow managed to grab hold of when no one was looking.

Altogether the most unsatisfactory encounter in the whole of our research.

Pl.xxv Holmanoid Krankenausener PIFFNITCH

THE VEGETABLE STENCHMAN

Deep inside every fridge there lurks a **Vegetable Stenchman**. He like to sit right at the bottom, often unperceived for several months, where he builds up an aroma so powerful that it has been known to strip heat-resistant tiles from the prow of the Space Shuttle. Sometimes its stench is so rife that whole countries have gone to war under the misapprehension that they were being attacked by chemical weapons. Indeed, once, a state of emergency was declared in Maryland, all because a Mrs. Elmer Symington opened her fridge door without warning the neighbours.

Yet the **Vegetable Stenchman** himself is a peace-loving, cheerful individual who likes nothing better than a chat about Latitude And Longitude, How To Tell Which Way Up A Ping-Pong Ball Is, and other fascinating topics of conversation. He can natter away for hours on the subject of Entertaining Fish Without Using Strong Language or How To Beguile Otters. If you meet him, try to draw him out on the subject of Where To Store Used Lollipop Sticks - you'll find he has some surprising answers.

Pl.xxvi The Vegetable STENCHMAN

LULU LITESHOCKER

Lulu Liteshocker one of the most playful and fun-loving of pong-producers. She is busy everywhere. Pongs in the garden, pongs in upstairs play-rooms, pongs in the cupboard where you keep the Christmas Decorations, pongs in unused lunch boxes, pongs behind the radiator, pongs under a bit of sack in the garage, she is constantly at work spreading laughter and merriment and producing surprising stinks and arresting aromas in the domestic environment.

Unfortunately, her personal life is rather questionable. It is rumoured that she once ran an illegal pong racket for the Mafia, and during prohibition in the States, she is said to have amassed a personal fortune producing whisky-like pongs for use in non-alcoholic drinks. When we tried to question her on this subject she grinned and lifted her legs in the air and produced a rather un-ladylike aroma from a portion of her anatomy that most young women keep to themselves.

Pl.xxvii Lulu LITESHOCKER

UNAMED SMELL SPRITE
possibly of the genus: Agalloch Agallocher

Rather surprisingly this is the **sprite** of joss-sticks. It actually produces some of the pleasantest smells to be found in the World of Olfaction, but it is, nonetheless, an unpleasant little creep. It has a deep knowledge of the nose and an understanding of scent that would make its fortune in the perfumeries of Paris, but it is insufferably rude and has as about as much social grace as a three-month old pizza.

It refers to people who light joss-sticks as "jossers" and affects to despize them as "pathetic hippie left-overs of the Sixties' drugs craze".

"That's what's wrong with this country," it told us, "it's never recovered from the pinko-socialist disaster of the sex-obsessed cup-cake lovers of pre-Thatcherite confectionery stores. What we need is a little more capital punishment and a little less Baked Alaska.* Give the middle classes and those that aspire to join them something to aim for - like motorised pencil sharpeners or designer buckets - and you'll soon turn the economy into a laundromat worth creaming designer jeans for."

We both decided that we didn't want to hear any more of this politically incomprehensible rubbish and we moved on.

* Baked Alaska - a kind of dessert - Ed. It's difficult to understand the sympathies or aspirations of this particular sprite. Politically it seems to be all over the place.

Pl.xxviii   Unamed Smell SPRITE

MATRICUS HUMIDICUS

One of the most mysterious of stains - the **Matricus Humidicus** always
remains damp. It is one of those stains that is impossible to dry-out.
No matter how much you air the sheets or dry out the offending rug,
the **Matricus Humidicus** remains moist.

    T.J.: To what do you attribute this extraordinary ability?

    M.H.: It is, Sir, merely a formula that was handed down to me
by my father. It was, I believe, an invention of *his* grandfather - a
Master Stain-Maker who had studied under the Great Dolap.

    T.J.: Who was the Great Dolap?

    M.H.: Ah...I see, Sir, you are not familiar with our world. The
Great Dellap Dolap, Sir, is the Father of our race or calling. He it
was, Sir, who first saw that there was a place for us in the world. In
the dark days that preceded him, stains, marks, blemishes, blotches,
smutches and their like were creatures of the shadow - ashamed of
themselves and of their own existence. They lived out their lives in
fear and self-loathing. The Great Dolap taught us to be proud of who
we were. He taught us that God created stains equal with those things
and creatures that abhor them. Nay, in some ways he had made us
superior, for when those creatures have passed on or passed away, we
stains remain. Sometimes we are the only evidence that those creatures
ever existed.

    The Great Dolap, Sir, foresaw a future in which maculations,
stains and smears would help guide and teach those thoughtless
creatures that now treat them so ill. He foresaw, Sir, a world in
which stains were understood and revered, where their beauty was
celebrated, and where their usefulness was utilized for the benefit
of all the world.

    T.J.: What happened to the Great Dolap?

    M.H.: Alas, Sir, martyred he was. The finest stain amongst us,
was taken to the cleaners some two thousand years ago, and suffered
the horrible fate that is the lot of so many of us. If that will be
all, Sir, perhaps you will excuse me..

And with that the Matricus Humidicus bowed and took his leave.

Pl.xxix Matricus HUMIDICUS

EMITTICUS ORIENTALIS WALLAH

Also known as *Effluvium Igneum* — literally "the smell that burns" — this little fellow is well-known to those of us who worship Mogul cuisine as it is celebrated in the Denmark Hill Tandoori, the Light of Bengal, the Khyber Pass, The Light of India, The Bombay Brasserie and thousands of like temples around the country. He is a friendly little stink, without malice but unaware of his own power. He comes to remind us of good times, of satisfied stomachs, of delicious flavours, of intense aromas and palate-tickling scents, but he brings with him the fire in the tail. The pleasure — all concentrated into one poignant moment the next morning — that is somehow too strong for us to hold onto.

Emitticus Orientalis Wallah also plays jazz trumpet — but only when no one is listening.

rites: "sibling enmity often starts in the
specially when the embryos are of different
of the male embryo to allow the female to
mb first or make sure she is sitting comfort-
he nine months of gestation can damage any

those ones wit
and unacknowl
number?

Now at las
hands a docume

relation-
ugh the
t of their
larly refusal
nale embryo
a game of
efore birth
natize the
mark him
ut all this is
.on — some
y worthless
n at that. In
the doctor
te it was not
octor and has
en imprisoned
ersonating a
officer.
The real ques-
s what was this
brother like?
sort of a man
he? Did he use
y matches or

Pl.xxx Emitticus Orientalis WALLAH

NAPTHOLUS SCOLASTICUS

An incorrigible little stain, which used to haunt the school-rooms of the world. Its behaviour was always wild and uncontrollable and it would appear everywhere - sometimes all at the same time - on pupils' hands, on their sleeves, all over their desks, on the floor. Teachers who tried to discipline it often found it adhering to their own gowns and fingers. It never seemed to learn anything, and every generation would claim it as their own. It would spring onto exercise books. It would hurl itself at fair copies of handwriting that had been specially executed for the Nation-Wide Hand-Writing Competition. It would fling itself over the cover of a text book just as the Headmaster was starting an inspection.

It was also the most stubborn of stains. Once it had found a spot it liked, it would stay there come wind or high water, soap suds or detergent. Many members of its family can still be seen, though faded through the years, on books in libraries up and down the country.

But, alas, Time moves on inexorably, even for stains, and now the **Naptholus** is a threatened species. The introduction of fountain pens was a severe blow followed a mere century later by the ball-point. Nowadays, of course, the word-processor has rung the final death knell. The **Naptholus** may cling on here or there in the studies of writers of science fiction or 18th century social historians, but its days are numbered as surely as Dr. Schone's Patent Sandals For The Deaf*.

*Another problem with Dr. Schone's Patent Sandals For The Deaf is that each one weighs over 300lbs and envelopes the whole foot to above the knee - making walking virtually impossible.

Pl.xxxi Naptholus SCOLASTICUS

SNAXGOBBER

The **Snaxgobber** can spit further than any other creature in the known (or unknown) Universe. His powers of expectoration are so prodigious and accurate than he can actually launch a bit of phlegm into orbit. Once in orbit, the phlegm will circle the Earth for a few years where it acts as a satellite for all Rupert Murdoch's TV channels. When it eventually returns to Earth, it breaks up into small fragments and covers all the cars in the area with sticky spots.

But the **Snaxgobber**'s talents are not confined to spitting. He can also gob up unbelievable quantities of ptyalism and dump it on unsuspecting passers-by. A favourite pastime of this unpleasant little character's is to stand on the roof of some public building, wait until a local dignitary comes along – perhaps to open a smart new stretch of urban motor-way or close-down some school or other, and then, as they pass beneath, he gobs anything up to thirty gallons of saliva and wallop! The shadow MP for Padstow or the Deputy Mayor of Toledo is covered in one of the least pleasant substances known to Man.

The saliva of the **Snaxgobber** has many peculiar qualities. Not only does it reduce all television transmissions to bland garbage (hence the problem with so much satellite and cable tv) but it also leaves a deep stain upon the psyche.

What is more, if the **Snaxgobber**'s sputum should chance to come into contact with newsprint, it immediately reacts to form an extremely unpleasant stain which appears to resemble a tabloid newspaper. It first forms itself into a red mast-head which reads: 'The Sun' or, occasionally, 'The New York Post,' and then forms the text and lots of pictures (preferably of young ladies with nothing on) to disguise the fact. As soon as you try to read it, however, you realize it is not a newspaper at all. It is in fact nothing more than a physical embodiment of the bile, prejudice, hatred and putrescence that goes to make up the **Snaxgobber**'s drool.

Pl.xxii Snax SNAXGOBBER

SAMANTHA SANITARIA

Samantha Sanitaria is a *unipungent* smell-sprite. That is to say she is capable of only producing one smell. It is the smell that haunts all hospitals, everywhere in the country, everywhere in the world. Whatever town or city, whatever nation, the moment you step through the doors of health into the world of illness, **Samantha** is there to greet you with her single odour. It doesn't matter whether the hospital is a general hospital, a maternity hospital, a geriatric hospital, a children's hospital, a military hospital or even a mental hospital, **Samantha** gives every one of them the same smell.

When we questioned her about her motives, she claimed that she was acting in the interests of the patients.

"It gives them a sense of security - of belonging. It reassures them that - whatever the building looks like - it *is* a genuine hospital. It's the same principle that lies behind the Holiday Inn chain of hotels. If you walked into a hospital and it smelt like a Roux Brothers' restaurant, or like a Paris brothel - you'd immediately start wondering if the staff really know what they're doing. But with my smell, pervading every corner, and every crack, seeping into every object that comes into the place - even the food - the patient is reassured and soothed."

We inquired why she didn't make it a pleasanter smell.

"Ah!" she replied. "*There's no point in encouraging malingerers to stay in hospital - especially if we're going to turn them into decent profit-making institutions...*"

We thanked her for her time, and moved on to the next subject.

Pl.xxxiii Samantha SANITARIA

DOGGITUS MUCILAGUS

One of the most familiar of stains — and yet one that is often invisible to the naked eye. One's first awareness of the presence of **Doggitus Mucilagus,** is the sensation of the sole of one's shoe sticking to the floor, or when running one's hand under a table in a restaurant one suddenly encounters that sticky patch that is impossible to explain by the Laws of Physics. Sometimes **Doggitus Mucilagus,** will suddenly appear around your fountain pen, or on the steering wheel of your car. There seems to be no credible explanation for how it got there.

    Doggitus works hard and discreetly but always mysteriously. He appears unexpectedly on the underside of the box your new watch came in, on page 32 of the paperback you've been reading for the last month, on the inside of the tea-cosy, halfway up a lavatory wall in Blairgowrie; he manifests himself on the handle of your knife that was perfectly clean a few moments ago, or on all the F-sharps on your Wurlitzer electric organ, on the back of the bus seat in front of you, on the wooden bench you've just sat on in the sauna, under the TV etc etc. And every time you look to see what has caused this unpleasant stickiness, there's never anything to see. Doggitus Mucilagus Mucilagus has slipped away again like a dream down the drain

Pl.xxxiv Doggitus MUCILAGUS

CYNOSURUS EPHEMERUS

One of the most extrovert of stains, the **Cynosurus Ephemerus** has no
sense of shame or false modesty. He besports himself with equal abandon
on the floors of embassies, across the entrance to the Club Class Lounge
at Heathrow, on the steps of smart night-spots, in the foyer of the
World Trade Centre, in the lift of the Dorchester Hotel, even on the
stairs of Buckingham Palace! He appears suddenly and gloriously and
completely unexpectedly. His arrival is instantly the cause of uproar
and apology. But his moment of glory is always short. For he is perhaps,
the most short-lived of all stains. He is gone within a few minutes of
his arrival. A lackey with a bucket and a mop gives him the *coup de
grace*, and he is no more than an unpleasant memory.

We asked him if he wouldn't prefer a more ~~a more~~ secure lifestyle.
"**Lor! Bless your stinky socks and body lice!**"
replied the **Cynosurus Ephemerus**.

"What would I be wanting with a dreary life in the shadows? I
wouldn't give a bachelor's fart for a whole day or even two whole days
on the floor of some miserable motel in Michigan! I tell you even a whole
week on a pavement outside a fish and chip shop in Skegness would mean
nothing to me! NO! Give to me the glorious life of notoriety in The
Groucho - no matter how short! I wouldn't swap one minute on Noel
Edmond's bathroom floor for a whole century of small-town obscurity!"

Pl.xxxv Cynosurus EPHEMERUS

OLFAXA FANNISOX &
THE REAL SMELL OF THE WORLD

Olfaxa Fannisox is revolted by any absence of pongs. She cannot abide the smell of the World when there are no external pongs **covering-up the Real Smell of the World. Th**us is revealed the paradox that has perplexed and bemused philosophers throughout the centuries. **What** *is the Real Smell of the World*?

In the Middle Ages it was believed that t**he Real Smell of the World existed only at** the cave known as Jacob's Bathroom in the Vale of Hebron. It was thought that if you went to the dead centre of this cave and put your nose to a particular crack, then and only then you would **be smelling the Real Smell of the World — unsullied by any other scent.**

Doubt was first thrown onto this idea by the Bishop of Devon in 1365, when he sugge**sted that perhaps the Real Smell of the World is to** be found in the Garden of Eden which was believed to be somewhere in Mesopotamia. He suggested a small cabbage patch near the town of Sanliurfa in Turkey. Travellers who made the long journey there in the Fourteenth Century reported back that if this w**as, indeed, the Real Smell of the World,** then the World was a smellier place than anyone had yet realised.

In the Fifteenth century, two Jesuit priests put forward the theory that the Garden of Eden had been mislocated and that it should have been roughly thirty miles to the south. They were burnt at the stake for this idea, and the wh**ole question of the Real Smell of the World was** shelved until 1978 when the Conference of Church Fathers sugg**ested that the Real Smell of the World** was simply a State of Mind which could be achieved by eating more radishes and leaving semolina out of your diet.

And so the controversy rages on to this very day. But one thing is certain: that it is only through **Olfaxa Fannisox** and her aversion to **the Real Smell of the World** that we know that it exists at all.

Pl.xxxvi Olfaxa Fannisox & THE REAL SMELL OF THE WORLD

THE GREAT STAIN OF THE APOCALYPSE

Finally, this is one stain we did not come across in our researches. Nor had any stain or smell-sprite we interviewed seen it. Yet they all expressed the conviction that it did exist.

Roughly speaking the general belief was of a Great Stain that would herald the End of Days. Some said it would be a Great Stain across the whole world - a stain that would s t r e t c h from the Arctic Sea to the mountains of Antarctica, from the Pacific Ocean to the China Sea. A stain that no mortal would be able to see except from space.

It sounds like a fairy tale, and yet, many of the pongs, sprites and blemishees that we interviewed firmly believed that it would one day come. Several described it to us, and it was remarkable how far the details they gave fitted each other. It is from these descriptions that Brian Froud was able to create this artist's impression of the Great Stain of the Apocalypse, with the fervent hope that none of us have to ever witness it in person.

Pl.xxxvii The Great Stain of the APOCALYPSE

PUBLISHER'S NOTICE

The views and opinions offered in this book are those of the stains and smell who give them and do not reflect the views or opinions of the publisher.

The publisher would also like to apologize for the inexplicable proliferation of stains which has occured during the printing of this book. Despite the great care taken during the printing process, further stains have unaccountably appeared on the pages facing the portraits of the stains and smells who were actually interviewed. The publisher would like to make it quite clear that these additional stains in no way represent shoddy workmanship, nor reduce the value of this book.